IMAGE OF THE GODS

IMAGE OF THE GODS

by Alan E. Nourse

It was nearly winter when the ship arrived. Pete Farnam never knew if the timing had been planned that way or not. It might have been coincidence that it came just when the colony was predicting its first real bumper crop of all time. When it was all over, Pete and Mario and the rest tried to figure it out, but none of them ever knew for sure just *what* had happened back on Earth, or *when* it had actually happened. There was too little information to go on, and practically none that they could trust. All Pete Farnam really knew, that day, was that this was the wrong year for a ship from Earth to land on Baron IV.

Pete was out on the plantation when it landed. As usual, his sprayer had gotten clogged; tarring should have been started earlier, before it got so cold that the stuff clung to the nozzle and hardened before the spray could settle into the dusty soil. The summer past had been the colony's finest in the fourteen years he'd been there, a warm, still summer with plenty of rain to keep the dirt down and let the *taaro* get well rooted and grow up tall and gray against the purple sky. But now the *taaro* was harvested. It was waiting, compressed and crated, ready for shipment, and the heavy black clouds were scudding nervously across the sky, faster with every passing day. Two days ago Pete had asked Mario to see about firing up the little furnaces the Dusties had built to help them fight the winter. All that remained now was tarring the fields, and then buckling down beneath the wind shields before the first winter storms struck.

Pete was trying to get the nozzle of the tar sprayer cleaned out when Mario's jeep came roaring down the rutted road from the village in a cloud of dust. In the back seat a couple of Dusties were bouncing up and down like happy five-year-olds. The brakes squealed and Mario bellowed at him from the road. "Pete! The ship's in! Better get hopping!"

Pete nodded and started to close up the sprayer. One of the Dusties tumbled out of the jeep and scampered across the field to give him a hand. It was an inexpert hand to say the least, but the Dusties seemed so proud of the little they were able to learn about mechanized farming that nobody had the heart to shoo them away. Pete watched the fuzzy brown creature get its paws thoroughly gummed up with tar before he pulled him loose and sent him back to the jeep with a whack on the backside. He finished the job himself, grabbed his coat from the back of the sprayer, and pulled himself into the front seat of the jeep.

Mario started the little car back down the road. The young colonist's face was coated with dust, emphasizing the lines of worry around his eyes. "I don't like it, Pete. There isn't any ship due this year."

"When did it land?"

"About twenty minutes ago. Won't be cool for a while yet."

Pete laughed. "Maybe Old Schooner is just getting lonesome to swap tall stories with us. Maybe he's even bringing us a locker of T-bones. Who knows?"

"Maybe," said Mario without conviction.

Pete looked at him, and shrugged. "Why complain if they're early? Maybe they've found some new way to keep our fields from blowing away on us every winter." He stared across at the heavy windbreaks between the fields—long, ragged structures built in hope of outwitting the vicious winds that howled across the land during the long winter. Pete picked bits of tar from his beard, and wiped the dirt from his forehead with the back of his hand. "This tarring is mean," he said wearily. "Glad to take a break."

"Maybe Cap Schooner will know something about the rumors we've been hearing," Mario said gloomily.

Pete looked at him sharply. "About Earth?"

Mario nodded. "Schooner's a pretty good guy, I guess. I mean, he'd tell us if anything was *really* wrong back home, wouldn't he?"

Pete nodded, and snapped his fingers. One of the Dusties hopped over into his lap and began gawking happily at the broad fields as the jeep jogged along. Pete stroked the creature's soft brown fur with his tar-caked fingers. "Maybe someday these little guys will show us where *they* go for the winter," he said. "They must have it down to a science."

Somehow the idea was funny, and both men roared. If the Dusties had *anything* down to a science, nobody knew what. Mario grinned and tweaked the creature's tail. "They sure do beat the winter, though," he said.

"So do we. Only we have to do it the human way. These fellas grew up in the climate." Pete lapsed into silence as the village came into view. The ship had landed quite a way out, resting on its skids on the long shallow groove the colonists had bulldozed out for it years before, the first year they had arrived on Baron IV. Slowly Pete turned Mario's words over in his mind, allowing himself to worry a little. There *had* been rumors of trouble back on Earth, persistent rumors he had taken care to soft-pedal, as mayor of the colony. There were other things, too, like the old newspapers and magazines that had been brought in by the lad from Baron II, and the rare radio message they could pick up through their atmospheric disturbance. Maybe something *was* going wrong back home. But somehow political upheavals on Earth seemed remote to these hardened colonists. Captain Schooner's visits were always welcome, but they were few and far between. The colony was small; one ship every three years could supply it, and even then the *taaro* crates wouldn't half fill up the storage holds. There were other colonies far closer to home that sent back more *taaro* in one year than Baron IV could grow in ten.

But when a ship did come down, it was a time of high excitement. It meant fresh food from Earth, meat from the frozen lockers, maybe even a little candy and salt. And always for Pete a landing meant a long evening of palaver with the captain about things back home and things on Baron IV.

Pete smiled to himself as he thought of it. He could remember Earth, of course, with a kind of vague nostalgia, but Baron IV was home to him now and he knew he would never leave it. He had too many hopes invested there, too many years of heartache and desperate hard work, too much deep satisfaction in having cut a niche for himself on this dusty, hostile world, ever to think much about Earth any more.

Mario stopped in front of the offices, and one of the Dusties hopped out ahead of Pete. The creature strode across the rough gravel to the door, pulling tar off his fingers just as he had seen Pete do. Pete followed him to the door, and then stopped, frowning. There should have been a babble of voices inside, with Captain Schooner's loud laugh roaring above the excitement. But Pete could hear nothing. A chill of uneasiness ran through him; he pushed open the door and walked inside. A dozen of his friends looked up silently, avoiding the eyes of the uniformed stranger in the center of the room. When he saw the man, Pete Farnam knew something was wrong indeed.

It wasn't Captain Schooner. It was a man he'd never seen before.

*

The Dustie ran across the room in front of Pete and hopped up on the desk as though he owned it, throwing his hands on his hips and staring at the stranger curiously. Pete took off his cap and parka and dropped them on a chair. "Well," he said. "This is a surprise. We weren't expecting a ship so soon."

The man inclined his head stiffly and glanced down at the paper he held in his hand. "You're Peter Farnam, I suppose? Mayor of this colony?"

"That's right. And you?"

"Varga is the name," the captain said shortly. "Earth Security and Supply." He nodded toward the small, frail-looking man in civilian clothes, sitting beside him. "This is Rupert Nathan, of the Colonial Service. You'll be seeing a great deal of him." He held out a small wallet of papers. "Our credentials, Farnam. Be so good as to examine them."

Pete glanced around the room. John Tegan and Hank Mario were watching him uneasily. Mary Turner was following the proceedings with her sharp little eyes, missing nothing, and Mel Dorfman stood like a rock, his heavy face curiously expressionless as he watched the visitors. Pete reached out for the papers, flipped through them, and handed them back with a long look at Captain Varga.

He was younger than Captain Schooner, with sandy hair and pale eyes that looked up at Pete from a soft baby face. Clean-shaven, his whole person seemed immaculate as he leaned back calmly in the chair. His civilian companion, however, had indecision written in every line of his pink face. His hands fluttered nervously, and he avoided the colonist's eyes.

Pete turned to the captain. "The papers say you're our official supply ship," he said. "You're early, but an Earth ship is always good

8

news." He clucked at the Dustie, who was about to go after one of the shiny buttons on the captain's blouse. The little brown creature hopped over and settled on Pete's knee. "We've been used to seeing Captain Schooner."

The captain and Nathan exchanged glances. "Captain Schooner has retired from Security Service," the captain said shortly. "You won't be seeing him again. But we have a cargo for your colony. You may send these people over to the ship to start unloading now, if you wish—" his eye swept the circle of windburned faces—"while Nathan and I discuss certain matters with you here."

Nobody moved for a moment. Then Pete nodded to Mario. "Take the boys out to unload, Jack. We'll see you back here in an hour or so."

"Pete, are you sure—"

"Don't worry. Take Mel and Hank along to lend a hand." Pete turned back to Captain Varga. "Suppose we go inside to more comfortable quarters," he said. "We're always glad to have word from Earth."

They passed through a dark, smelly corridor into Pete's personal quarters. For a colony house, if wasn't bad—good plastic chairs, a hand-made rug on the floor, even one of Mary Turner's paintings on the wall, and several of the weird, stylized carvings the Dusties had done for Pete. But the place smelled of tar and sweat, and Captain Varga's nose wrinkled in distaste. Nathan drew out a large silk handkerchief and wiped his pink hands, touching his nose daintily.

The Dustie hopped into the room ahead of them and settled into the biggest, most comfortable chair. Pete snapped his fingers sharply, and the brown creature jumped down again like a naughty child and climbed up on Pete's knee. The captain glanced at the chair with disgust and sat down in another. "Do you actually let those horrid creatures have the run of your house?" he asked.

"Why not?" Pete said. "We have the run of their planet. They're quite harmless, really. And quite clean."

The captain sniffed. "Nasty things. Might find a use for the furs, though. They look quite soft."

"We don't kill Dusties," said Pete coolly. "They're friendly, and intelligent too, in a childish sort of way." He looked at the captain and Nathan, and decided not to put on the coffee pot. "Now what's the trouble?"

"No trouble at all," the captain said, "except the trouble you choose to make. You have your year's *taaro* ready for shipping?"

"Of course."

The captain took out a small pencil on a chain and began to twirl it. "How much, to be exact?"

"Twenty thousand, Earth weight."

"Tons?"

Pete shook his head. "Hundredweight."

The captain raised his eyebrows. "I see. And there are—" he consulted the papers in his hand—"roughly two hundred and twenty colonists here on Baron IV. Is that right?"

"That's right."

"Seventy-four men, eighty-one women, and fifty-nine children, to be exact?"

"I'd have to look it up. Margaret Singman had twins the other night."

"Well, don't be ridiculous," snapped the captain. "On a planet the size of Baron IV, with seventy-four men, you should be producing a dozen times the *taaro* you stated. We'll consider that your quota for a starter, at least. You have ample seed, according to my records. I should think, with the proper equipment—"

"Now wait a minute," Pete said softly. "We're fighting a climate here, captain. You should know that. We have only a two-planting season, and the 'proper equipment,' as you call it, doesn't operate too well out here. It has a way of clogging up with dust in the summer, and rusting in the winter."

"Really," said Captain Varga. "As I was saying, with the proper equipment, you could cultivate a great deal more land than you seem to be using. This would give you the necessary heavier yield. Wouldn't you say so, Nathan?"

The little nervous man nodded. "Certainly, captain. With the proper organization of labor."

"That's nonsense," Pete said, suddenly angry. "Nobody can get that kind of yield from this planet. The ground won't give it, and the men won't grow it."

The captain gave him a long look. "Really?" he said. "I think you're wrong. I think the men will grow it."

Pete stood up slowly. "What are you trying to say? This business about quotas and organization of labor—"

"You didn't read our credentials as we instructed you, Farnam. Mr. Nathan is the official governor of the colony on Baron IV, as of now. You'll find him most co-operative, I'm sure, but he's answerable directly to me in all matters. My job is administration of the entire Baron system. Clear enough?"

Pete's eyes were dark. "I think you'd better draw me a picture," he said tightly. "A very clear picture."

"Very well. Baron IV is not paying for its upkeep. *Taaro*, after all, is not the most necessary of crops in the universe. It has value, but not very much value, all things considered. If the production of *taaro* here is not increased sharply, it may be necessary to close down the colony altogether."

"You're a liar," said Pete shortly. "The Colonization Board makes no production demands on the colonies. Nor does it farm out systems for personal exploitation."

The captain smiled. "The Colonization Board, as you call it, has undergone a slight reorganization," he said.

"*Reorganization!* It's a top-level board in the Earth Government! Nothing could reorganize it but a wholesale—" He broke off, his jaw sagging as the implication sank in.

"You're rather out on a limb, you see," said the captain coolly. "Poor communications and all that. The fact is that the entire Earth Government has undergone a slight reorganization also."

*

The Dustie knew that something had happened.

Pete didn't know how he knew. The Dusties couldn't talk, couldn't make *any* noise, as far as Pete knew. But they always seemed to know when something unusual was happening. It was wrong, really, to consider them unintelligent animals. There are other sorts of intelligence than human, and other sorts of communication, and other sorts of culture. The Baron IV colonists had never understood the queer perceptive sense that the Dusties seemed to possess, any more than they knew how many Dusties there were, or what they ate, or where on the planet they lived. All they knew was that when they landed on Baron IV, the Dusties were there.

At first the creatures had been very timid. For weeks the men and women, busy with their building, had paid little attention to the skittering brown forms that crept down from the rocky hills to watch them with big, curious eyes. They were about half the size of men, and strangely humanoid in appearance, not in the sense that a monkey is humanoid (for they did *not* resemble monkeys) but in some way the colonists could not quite pin down. It may have been the way they walked around on their long, fragile hind legs, the way they stroked their pointed chins as they sat and watched and listened with their pointed ears lifted alertly, watching with soft gray eyes, or the way they handled objects with their little four-fingered hands. They were so remarkably human-like in their elfin way that the colonists couldn't help but be drawn to the creatures.

That whole first summer, when the colonists were building the village and the landing groove for the ships, the Dusties were among them, trying pathetically to help, so eager for friendship that even occasional rebuffs failed to drive them away. They *liked* the colony. They seemed, somehow, to savor the atmosphere, moving about like solemn, fuzzy overseers as the work progressed through the summer. Pete Farnam thought that they had even tried to warn the people about the winter. But the colonists couldn't understand, of course. Not until later. The Dusties became a standing joke, and were tolerated with considerable amusement—until the winter struck.

It had come with almost unbelievable ferocity. The houses had not been completed when the first hurricanes came, and they were smashed into toothpicks. The winds came, vicious winds full of dust and sleet and ice, wild erratic twisting gales that ripped the village to shreds, tearing off the topsoil that had been broken and fertilized—merciless, never-ending winds that wailed and screamed the planet's protest. The winds drove sand and dirt and ice into the heart of the generators, and the heating units corroded and jammed and went dead. The jeeps and tractors and bulldozers were scored and rusted. The people began dying by the dozens as they huddled down in the pitiful little pits they had dug to try to keep the winds away.

Few of them were still conscious when the Dusties had come silently, in the blizzard, eyes closed tight against the blast, to drag the people up into the hills, into caves and hollows that still showed the fresh marks of carving tools. They had brought food—what kind of food nobody knew, for the colony's food had been destroyed by the first blast of the hurricane—but whatever it was it had kept them alive. And somehow, the colonists had survived the winter which seemed never to end. There were frozen legs and ruined eyes; there was pneumonia so swift and virulent that even the antibiotics they managed to salvage could not stop it; there was near-starvation—but they were kept alive, until the winds began to die, and they walked out of their holes in the ground to see the ruins of their first village.

From that winter on, nobody considered the Dusties funny any more. What had motivated them no one knew, but the colony owed them their lives. The Dusties tried to help the people rebuild. They showed them how to build windshields that would keep houses intact and anchored to the ground when the winds came again. They built little furnaces out of dirt and rock which defied the winds and gave great heat. They showed the colonists a dozen things they needed to know for life on the rugged planet. The colonists in turn tried to teach the Dusties something about Earth, and how the colonists had lived, and why they had come. But there was a barrier of intelligence that could not be crossed. The Dusties learned simple things, but only slowly and imperfectly. They seemed content to take on their mock overseer's role, moving in and about the village, approving or disapproving, but always trying to help. Some became personal pets, though "pet" was the wrong word, because it was more of a strange personal friendship limited by utter lack of communication, than any animal-and-master relationship. The colonists made sure that the Dusties were granted the respect due them as rightful masters of Baron IV. And somehow the Dusties perceived this attitude, and were so grateful for the acceptance and friendship that there seemed nothing they wouldn't do for the colonists.

There had been many discussions about them. "You'd think they'd resent our moving in on them," Jack Mario had said one day. "After all, we *are* usurpers. And they treat us like kings. Have you noticed the way they mimic us? I saw one chewing tobacco the other day. He hated the stuff, but he chewed away, and spat like a trooper."

One of the Dusties had been sitting on Pete's knee when Captain Varga had been talking, and he had known that something terrible was wrong. Now he sat on the desk in the office, moving uneasily back and forth as Pete looked up at Mario's dark face, and then across at John Tegan and Mel Dorfman. John's face was dark with anger as he ran his fingers through the heavy gray beard that fell to his chest. Mel sat stunned, shaking his head helplessly. Mario was unable to restrain himself. His face was bitter as he stomped across the room, then returned to shake his fist under Pete's nose. "But did you see him?" he choked. "Governor of the colony! What does he know about growing *taaro* in this kind of soil? Did you see those hands? Soft, dainty, pink! How could a man with hands like that govern a colony?"

Pete looked over at John Tegan. "Well, John?"

The big man looked up, his eyes hollow under craggy brows. "It's below the belt, Pete. But if the government's been overthrown, then the captain is right. It leaves us out on a limb."

Pete shook his head. "*I* can't give him an answer," he said. "The answer has got to come from the colony. All I can do is speak for the colony."

Tegan stared at the floor. "We're an Earth colony," he said softly. "I know that. I was born in New York. I lived there for many years. But Earth isn't my home any more. This is." He looked at Pete. "I built it, and so did you. All of us built it, even when things were getting stormy back home. Maybe that's why we came, maybe somehow we saw the handwriting on the wall."

"But when did it happen?" Mel burst out suddenly. "How could *anything* so big happen so fast?"

14

"Speed was the secret," Pete said gloomily. "It was quick, it was well organized, and the government was unstable. We're just caught in the edge of it. Pity the ones living there, now. But the new government considers the colonies as areas for exploitation instead of development."

"Well, they can't do it," Mario cried. "This is *our* land, *our* home. Nobody can tell us what to grow in our fields."

Pete's fist slammed down on the desk. "Well, how are you going to stop them? The law of the land is sitting out there in that ship. Tomorrow morning he's coming back here to install his fat little friend as governor. He has guns and soldiers on that ship to back him up. What are you going to do about it?"

"Fight it," Mario said.

"How?"

Jack Mario looked around the room. "There are only a dozen men on that ship," he said softly. "We've got seventy-four. When Varga comes back to the village tomorrow, we tell him to take his friend back to the ship and shove off. We give him five minutes to get turned around, and if he doesn't, we start shooting."

"Just one little thing," said Pete quietly. "What about the supplies? Even if we fought them off and won, what about the food, the clothing, the replacement parts for the machines?"

"We don't need machinery to farm this land," said Mario eagerly. "There's food here, food we can live on; the Dusties showed us that the first winter. And we can farm the land for our own use and let the machinery rust. There's nothing they can bring us from Earth that we can't do without."

"We couldn't get away with it!" Mel Dorfman shook his head bitterly. "You're asking us to cut ourselves off from Earth completely. But they'd never let us. They'd send ships to bomb us out."

"We could hide, and rebuild after they had finished."

Pete Farnam sighed. "They'd never leave us alone, Jack. Didn't you see that captain? His kind of mind can't stand opposition. We'd just be a thorn in the side of the new Earth Government. They don't want *any* free colonies."

"Well, let's give them one." Mario sat down tiredly, snapping his fingers at the Dustie. "Furs!" he snarled. He looked up, his dark eyes burning. "It's no good, Pete. We can't let them get away with it. Produce for them, yes. Try to raise the yield for them, yes. But not a governor. If they insist on that we can throw them out, and keep them out."

"I don't think so. They'd kill every one of us first."

John Tegan sat up, and looked Pete Farnam straight in the eye. "In that case, Peter, it might just be better if they did."

Pete stared at him for a moment and slowly stood up. "All right," he said. "Call a general colony meeting. We'll see what the women think. Then we'll make our plans."

*

The ship's jeep skidded to a halt in a cloud of dust. Captain Varga peered through the windshield. Then he stood up, staring at the three men blocking the road at the edge of the village. The little pink-faced man at his side turned white when he saw their faces, and his fingers began to tremble. Each of the men had a gun.

"You'd better clear the road," the captain snapped. "We're driving through."

Pete Farnam stepped forward. He pointed to Nathan. "Take your friend there back to the ship. Leave him there. We don't want him here."

Nathan turned to Varga. "I told you," he said viciously. "Too big for their boots. Go on through."

The captain laughed and gunned the motor, started straight for the men blocking the road. Then Jack Mario shot a hole in his front tire. The jeep lurched to a stop. Captain Varga stood up, glaring at the men. "Farnam, step out here," he said.

"You heard us," Pete said, without moving. "Crops, yes. We'll try to increase our yield. But no overseer. Leave him here and we'll kill him."

"Once more," said the captain, "clear the way. This man is your new governor. He will be regarded as the official agent of the Earth Government until the final production capacity of this colony is determined. Now clear out."

16

The men didn't move. Without another word, the captain threw the jeep into reverse, jerked back in a curve, and started the jeep, flat tire and all, back toward the ship in a billow of dust.

Abruptly the village exploded into activity. Four men took up places behind the row of windbreaks beyond the first row of cabins. Pete turned and ran back into the village. He found John Tegan commandeering a squad of ten dirty-faced men. "Are the women and children all out?" he shouted.

"All taken care of." Tegan spat tobacco juice, and wiped his mouth with the back of his hand.

"Where's Mel?"

"Left flank. He'll try to move in behind them. Gonna be tough, Pete, they've got good weapons."

"What about the boys last night?"

John was checking the bolt on his ancient rifle. "Hank and Ringo? Just got back an hour ago. If Varga wants to get his surface planes into action, he's going to have to dismantle them and rebuild them outside. The boys jammed up the launching ports for good." He spat again. "Don't worry, Pete. This is going to be a ground fight."

"Okay." Pete held out his hand to the old man. "This may be it. And if we turn them back, there's bound to be more later."

"There's a lot of planet to hide on," said Tegan. "They may come back, but after a while they'll go again."

Pete nodded. "I just hope we'll still be here when they do."

They waited. It seemed like hours. Pete moved from post to post among the men, heavy-faced men he had known all his life, it seemed. They waited with whatever weapons they had available—pistols, home-made revolvers, ortho-guns, an occasional rifle, even knives and clubs. Pete's heart sank. They were bitter men, but they were a mob with no organization, no training for fighting. They would be facing a dozen of Security's best-disciplined shock troops, armed with the latest weapons from Earth's electronics laboratories. The colonists didn't stand a chance.

Pete got his rifle and made his way up the rise of ground overlooking the right flank of the village. Squinting, he could spot the cloud of dust rising up near the glistening ship, moving toward the village. And then, for the first time, he realized that he hadn't seen any Dusties all day.

It puzzled him. They had been in the village in abundance an hour before dawn, while the plans were being laid out. He glanced around, hoping to see one of the fuzzy brown forms at his elbow, but he saw nothing. And then, as he stared at the cloud of dust coming across the valley, he thought he saw the ground moving.

He blinked, and rubbed his eyes. With a gasp he dragged out his binoculars and peered down at the valley floor. There were thousands of them, hundreds of thousands, their brown bodies moving slowly out from the hills surrounding the village, converging into a broad, liquid column between the village and the ship. Even as he watched, the column grew thicker, like a heavy blanket being drawn across the road, a multitude of Dusties lining up.

Pete's hair prickled on the back of his neck. They knew so little about the creatures, so *very* little. As he watched the brown carpet rolling out, he tried to think. Could there be a weapon in their hands, could they somehow have perceived the evil that came from the ship, somehow sensed the desperation in the men's voices as they had laid their plans? Pete stared, a sinking feeling in the pit of his stomach. They were there in the road, thousands upon thousands of them, standing there, waiting—for what?

Three columns of dust were coming from the road now. Through the glasses Pete could see the jeeps, filled with men in their gleaming gray uniforms, crash helmets tight about their heads, blasters glistening in the pale light. They moved in deadly convoy along the rutted road, closer and closer to the crowd of Dusties overflowing the road.

The Dusties just stood there. They didn't move. They didn't shift, or turn. They just waited.

The captain's car was first in line. He pulled up before the line with a screech of brakes, and stared at the sea of creatures before him. "Get out of there!" he shouted.

The Dusties didn't move.

The captain turned to his men. "Fire into them," he snapped. "Clear a path."

There was a blaze of fire, and a half a dozen Dusties slid to the ground, convulsing. Pete felt a chill pass through him, staring in disbelief. The Dusties had a weapon, he kept telling himself, they *must* have a weapon, something the colonists had never dreamed of. The guns came up again, and another volley echoed across the valley, and a dozen more Dusties fell to the ground. For every one that fell, another moved stolidly into its place.

With a curse the captain sat down in the seat, gunned the motor, and started forward. The jeep struck the fallen bodies, rolled over them, and plunged straight into the wall of Dusties. Still they didn't move. The car slowed and stopped, mired down. The other cars picked up momentum and plunged into the brown river of creatures. They too ground to a stop.

The captain started roaring at his men. "Cut them down! We're going to get through here!" Blasters began roaring into the faces of the Dusties, and as they fell the jeeps moved forward a few feet until more of the creatures blocked their path.

Pete heard a cry below him, and saw Jack Mario standing in the road, gun on the ground, hands out in front of him, staring in horror as the Dusties kept moving into the fire. "Do you see what they're doing!" he screamed. "They'll be slaughtered, every one of them!" And then he was running down the road, shouting at them to stop, and so were Pete and Tegan and the rest of the men.

Something hit Pete in the shoulder as he ran. He spun around and fell into the dusty road. A dozen Dusties closed in around him, lifted him up bodily, and started back through the village with him. He tried to struggle, but vaguely he saw that the other men were being carried back also, while the river of brown creatures held the jeeps at bay. The Dusties were hurrying, half carrying and half dragging him back through the village and up a long ravine into the hills beyond. At last they set Pete on his feet again, plucking urgently at his shirt sleeve as they hurried him along.

He followed them willingly, then, with the rest of the colonists at his heels. He didn't know what the Dusties were doing, but he knew they were trying to save him. Finally they reached a cave, a great cleft in the rock that Pete knew for certain had not been there when he had led exploring parties through these hills years before. It was a huge opening, and already a dozen of the men were there, waiting, dazed by what they had witnessed down in the valley, while more were stumbling up the rocky incline, tugged along by the fuzzy brown creatures.

Inside the cavern, steps led down the side of the rock, deep into the dark coolness of the earth. Down and down they went, until they suddenly found themselves in a mammoth room lit by blazing torches. Pete stopped and stared at his friends who had already arrived. Jack Mario was sitting on the floor, his face in his hands, sobbing. Tegan was sitting, too, blinking at Pete as if he were a stranger, and Dorfman was trembling like a leaf. Pete stared about him through the dim light, and then looked where Tegan was pointing at the end of the room.

He couldn't see it clearly, at first. Finally, he made out a raised platform with four steps leading up. A torch lighted either side of a dais at the top, and between the torches, rising high into the gloom, stood a statue.

It was a beautifully carved thing, hewn from the heavy granite that made up the core of this planet, with the same curious styling as other carving the Dusties had done. The design was intricate, the lines carefully turned and polished. At first Pete thought it was a statue of a Dustie, but when he moved forward and squinted in the dim light, he suddenly realized that it was something else indeed. And in that moment he realized why they were there and why the Dusties had done this incredible thing to protect them.

The statue was weirdly beautiful, the work of a dedicated master sculptor. It was a figure, standing with five-fingered hands on hips, head raised high. Not a portrait, but an image seen through other eyes than human, standing high in the room with the lights burning reverently at its feet.

Unmistakably it was the statue of a man.

*

They heard the bombs, much later. The granite roof and floor of the cavern trembled, and the men and women stared at each other, helpless and sick as they huddled in that great hall. But presently the bombing stopped. Later, when they stumbled out of that grotto into the late afternoon light, the ship was gone.

They knew it would be back. Possibly it would bring back search parties to hunt down the rebels in the hills; perhaps it would just wait and again bomb out the new village when it rose. But searching parties would never find their quarry, and the village would rise again and again, if necessary.

And in the end, somehow, Pete knew that the colonists would find a way to survive here and live free as they had always lived. It might be a bitter struggle, but no matter how hard the fight, there would be one strange and wonderful thing they could count on.

No matter what they had to do, he knew the Dusties would help them.